EARTH'S GOT TALENT!

For Evan, Taylor, and Jordan, with glorbs of woogak
(translation: lots of love)
—L.H.H.

For my superstar sister Eva, my childhood
singing buddy who taught me to project
—J.W.

Text copyright © 2016 by Lori Haskins Houran
Illustrations copyright © 2016 by Jessica Warrick
Galaxy Scout Activities illustrations copyright © 2016 by Kane Press, Inc.
Galaxy Scout Activities illustrations by Nadia DiMattia

Library of Congress Cataloging-in-Publication Data

Houran, Lori Haskins.
Earth's got talent! / by Lori Haskins Houran ; illustrated by Jessica Warrick.
  pages   cm. — (How to be an earthling ; 4)
Summary: In Mrs. Buckle's class, which includes Spork the alien, shy Grace
wants to find the courage to perform a solo at the talent show, but her best
friend needs her as a magician's assistant.
ISBN 978-1-57565-828-5 (pbk) — ISBN 978-1-57565-827-8 (reinforced library
binding) — ISBN 978-1-57565-829-2 (ebook)
[1. Extraterrestrial beings—Fiction. 2. Talent show—Fiction. 3. Courage—Fiction.
4. Schools—Fiction. 5. Humorous stories.] I. Warrick, Jessica, illustrator. II. Title.
III. Title: Earth has got talent.
PZ7.H27645Ear 2016
[Fic]—dc23
2015023476

3 5 7 9 10 8 6 4 2

First published in the United States of America in 2016 by Kane Press, Inc.
Printed in China

Book Design: Edward Miller

How to Be an Earthling is a trademark of Kane Press, Inc.

Visit us online at **www.kanepress.com**

 Like us on Facebook
facebook.com/kanepress

 Follow us on Twitter
@KanePress

CONTENTS

1. Earth to Grace 11

2. Got Talent? 17

3. Mountains and

    Monkey Bars 24

4. Hocus Pocus 34

5. The Show Must Go On 44

    Galaxy Scout Activities............ 58

**Don't miss a single one
of Spork's adventures!**

Spork Out of Orbit

Greetings, Sharkling!

Take Me to Your Weeder

Earth's Got Talent!

No Place Like Space

Alien in the Outfield

May the Votes Be with You

Money Doesn't Grow on Mars

EARTH'S GOT TALENT!

by Lori Haskins Houran
illustrated by Jessica Warrick

KANE PRESS
New York

Spork

Trixie Lopez

Mrs. Buckle

Jack Donnelly

Grace Hanford

Jo Jo

Newton Miller

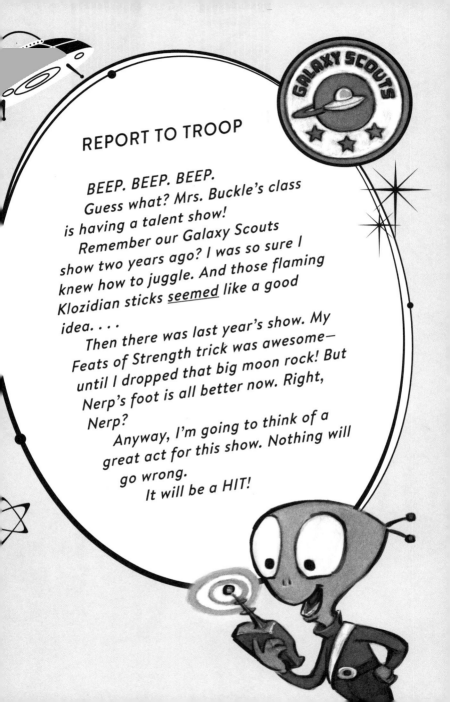

REPORT TO TROOP

BEEP. BEEP. BEEP.
Guess what? Mrs. Buckle's class is having a talent show!

Remember our Galaxy Scouts show two years ago? I was so sure I knew how to juggle. And those flaming Klozidian sticks <u>seemed</u> like a good idea. . . .

Then there was last year's show. My Feats of Strength trick was awesome—until I dropped that big moon rock! But Nerp's foot is all better now. Right, Nerp?

Anyway, I'm going to think of a great act for this show. Nothing will go wrong.

It will be a HIT!

1

EARTH TO GRACE

"Don't forget—the talent show is on Monday," said Mrs. Buckle. "You have four more days to work on your acts. I can't wait to see what you do!"

Grace felt a flutter in her belly. Forget the talent show? It was all she'd thought about since Mrs. Buckle announced it!

The bell rang, and the class spilled into the hallway.

"I know what *I'm* doing for the show," said Jack. "Karate. Hi-YAH!" He chopped the air with his hands.

"I'm going to play the clarinet," said Newton. "That's what I did at my camp talent show last summer. How about you, Spork? Were you ever in a talent show on your planet?"

"Er, yes," said the little alien. "But I think I'll do something different this time!" Then he frowned. "I don't know what, though."

Grace was quiet. She knew exactly what she wanted to do for the show. She just wasn't sure she was brave enough.

A few weeks ago, Grace had made a surprising discovery. Well, two discoveries. First, she and her classmates had found Spork when his spaceship landed at their school! That was a surprise for everyone.

Grace had made the second discovery on her own. She was in her room, singing along to the radio, when the power went out. The music stopped, but Grace kept singing loudly—and her voice sounded just as good as the one on the radio!

After that, Grace started singing every day. She *loved* it. When she closed her eyes and let her voice climb higher and higher, she felt as if she were flying!

She hadn't dared to sing in front of anyone yet. Or even to tell anyone about her singing—including Trixie, her best friend.

Maybe, Grace thought, *it doesn't have to be a secret anymore.*

Grace pictured herself at the talent show. She saw herself stand up tall, open her mouth, and—

"HELLO! EARTH TO GRACE!" yelled

Trixie. "I've got it. The perfect thing for
us to do at the show!"

"Us?" said Grace.

"Of course!" said Trixie impatiently.
"We'll do a magic act. I'll be the Amazing
Magician, and you'll be my Helpful
Assistant. I'll saw you in half!"

"Oh," said Grace. "It's just . . . um . . ."

"What, no sawing? We can talk about that. But it will be great, right?"

"It *would* be great, but—"

"Awesome!" said Trixie. "Come over on Saturday to practice."

Grace sighed. It was no use arguing with Trixie.

Besides, who am I kidding? I'm the shyest person in the class! Grace thought. *I could never sing in front of everyone!*

Except deep down, she thought that maybe—just *maybe*—she could.

2

GOT TALENT?

Grace watched Trixie climb onto the
school bus.

Grace didn't ride the bus. Her house
was right next door to the school. Spork
didn't ride it either. His ship was still
parked on the school playground!

They liked to walk home together,
even if it only took a minute. Usually
Spork was full of questions for Grace.

He had been on Earth for three weeks now, but there were still things that puzzled him. Like, *Why can't Earth chickens fly?* And, *Why did Earthlings invent frozen yogurt when Earth ice cream is so good?*

Today, Spork was quiet.

"Are you okay?" asked Grace.

"I have a problem," Spork said. "About the talent show."

"Me too!" said Grace.

They looked at each other in surprise.

"What's your problem?" Grace asked.

"My talent," said Spork. "I don't have one!"

They reached Spork's spaceship. Spork pulled a lever. *ZZZT!* A panel slid

open. *PING!* A shiny silver step popped
out.

Grace and Spork sat down.

"Are you sure?" Grace said.
"I bet you have lots
of talents."

"Not really," said Spork. "The stuff I can do is just . . . ordinary."

"Why don't you show me?" Grace suggested.

"All right. But it's nothing special."

Spork took a piece of gum out of his pocket. He chewed it a few times. Then he blew a bubble . . . from his ear!

"Wow!" said Grace. "I've never seen anyone do that!"

"Really?" said Spork. "Everyone on my planet can blow bubbles."

Next Spork held his breath. After a few seconds he started to change color. He flashed from orange to blue to green!

"That's COOL!" Grace yelped.

"It is?" said Spork. "You know, if I keep going, I can get all the way to purple."

"Spork, that stuff might be ordinary on your planet. But here it's . . . *extraordinary*!" said Grace.

"I almost forgot! I can do one more thing." Spork closed one eye. "I can WINK!"

"Oh. Earthlings can do that, too."
Grace winked back at Spork. "But the
other things are amazing!"

"Thanks!" Spork looked happier now.
"It's not enough for a whole act, but it's
a start. So what's *your* problem, Grace?
I thought you and Trixie already had an
act."

Grace nodded. "I kind of want to do
something else. But I can't tell Trixie."

"Why not?" asked Spork.

"Well . . . ," said Grace.

She wasn't sure how to explain it.
Grace loved being best friends with
Trixie. Trixie was the most fun kid in
third grade. But Trixie was always in
charge. When they played White House,
Trixie was the President and Grace was

the Vice President. When they played Family, Trixie was the big sister and Grace was the little sister—even though Grace was two months and three days older.

Normally Grace didn't mind. It was easy following Trixie's lead. But now Grace wanted to do something her own way.

Or did she?

She pictured herself again at the talent show. This time she wasn't standing tall. Instead, she was staring at the ground. She looked small and scared.

"Never mind," Grace said sadly. She stood up to go. "It was a dumb idea anyway."

3

MOUNTAINS AND MONKEY BARS

"I've got it all planned out!" Trixie said the next morning. She leaned over Grace's desk. "We'll start with a card trick. You'll pick a card, and I'll guess what it is. Then you'll hold a hat, and I'll pull a rabbit out of it. No—I'll pull *Jo Jo* out of it!"

Grace looked over at Jo Jo, nibbling her hamster food in her tank.

"If you don't want me to saw you in half, that's fine. I'll make you disappear or something. Grace, are you listening?"

Grace nodded. But she was glad when Mrs. Buckle clapped her hands for attention.

"Good morning!" Mrs. Buckle called. "It's Friday, so let's start with an Incredible Kids video."

"Yay!" said Trixie.

Grace liked these videos, too. They showed kids from all over the world doing amazing things. Last week there was a girl who trained horses—and before that, a boy who built computers.

"Malavath Purna was just thirteen years

old when she climbed Mount Everest," the voice on the video said.

A girl's face filled the screen. She had long, dark hair and a wide smile.

"The climb was dangerous and difficult. Malavath and her team faced blizzards and subzero temperatures."

Brr! Grace shivered just looking at the snow-covered mountain.

"At times she was tired, cold, and very afraid. But she told herself, 'I will not let fear stop me. I will not give up.' After fifty-two days, Malavath reached the top. She became the youngest girl ever to climb the world's highest mountain!"

The video ended with Malavath on top of Mount Everest. Her smile was

even wider than before, and her eyes
were shining.

"What do you think?" said Mrs.
Buckle.

"I like it!" said Spork. "But I don't
think I want to climb Mount Everest. I'd
rather take my spaceship to the top!"

Mrs. Buckle smiled. "Anyone else?"

Grace raised her hand. "Malavath was really brave," she said.

"She didn't sound brave to me," scoffed Jack. "I mean, she admitted she was scared, right?"

"That's an interesting point, Jack," Mrs. Buckle said. "But courage doesn't mean you're not afraid. Courage means you do something even though you *are* afraid."

"Fine," Jack muttered. "I still wouldn't admit it!"

The class moved on to Morning Math. But Grace couldn't stop thinking about Malavath and the mountain.

"I will not let fear stop me. I will not give up." The video played in Grace's mind

all through Language Arts. She couldn't even focus on the spelling bee.

"*Weird,*" she said. "*W-I-E-R-D.*"

"Not quite," said Mrs. Buckle. "Are you all right, Grace?"

"Yes, Mrs. Buckle," mumbled Grace.

By recess she had made up her mind. She was going to be like Malavath. She wasn't going to let fear stop her. She was going to sing in the show!

But first, she had to face another fear.

"Trixie?" she said. "I have to tell you something."

"What is it?" Trixie was hanging from the monkey bars by her knees.

Grace gulped. "I can't be your assistant at the talent show."

"WHAT?" said Trixie. "Why not?"

"Because I want to do something else."

Grace watched Trixie's face turn red. She wasn't sure if it was because Trixie was mad or because she was upside-down.

Trixie flipped to the ground. Her face got even redder than before.

"I can't do a magic act by myself!" she said. "Who's going to pick a card? Who's going to hold the hat?"

Grace felt awful. Maybe she was being unfair. Maybe she should just do what Trixie wanted. It would be a lot easier that way.

Then she thought of Malavath again. *"I will not let fear stop me. I will not give up."*

"I'm really sorry, Trixie," Grace said softly.

Trixie didn't say a word. She stomped away.

"Grace, what's going on?" asked Spork, hurrying over.

Grace looked at the alien's worried face. Then she got an idea!

"I'm not doing the act with Trixie," she said. "But *you* should, Spork! Nobody knows what you can do—the ear bubble and stuff. You and Trixie could turn it into a magic act. You'd be a hit!"

"A *hit*?" said Spork. "I'll go ask Trixie right now!"

He sped off. From across the

playground, Grace watched Trixie give him a high-five.

Grace felt a little better. Spork's problem was solved. Trixie's problem was solved.

But now Grace had two problems of her own, and she didn't know which one was bigger. Singing in front of the class . . . or getting her best friend back.

4

HOCUS POCUS

The weekend flew by. Grace practiced and practiced—and worried and worried!

But now it was Monday morning and time for the show. Grace felt calm. She looked around the classroom. She had known these kids since kindergarten. And Spork already felt like an old friend.

Everyone will be nice about my singing, she told herself. *Well, maybe not Jack.*

She caught Trixie's eye. Trixie turned away.

And maybe not Trixie.

"Listen up!" Mrs. Buckle said. She looked excited. "I just saw Principal Hale. She invited us to perform our show on the cafeteria stage." Mrs. Buckle paused. *"For the whole school!"*

"Yahoo!" yelled Jack. "Wait till everyone sees my moves!"

"My sister's in kindergarten. She'll get to hear me play!" Newton said.

"Gather up your things, and we'll head down there," said Mrs. Buckle.

All around Grace, kids started scrambling. Newton grabbed his clarinet. Trixie pulled a purple cape out of her backpack.

Grace didn't budge.

"The whole school?" she whispered.

"Come on," said Spork, pulling her hand. "Let's go!"

Mrs. Buckle's class sat down at a table next to the stage. The cafeteria was already filled with kids. All the teachers were there, too. Mr. Albert, the custodian, was chatting with the school cook, Mrs. Reese.

"The whole school," Grace whispered again.

Principal Hale dimmed the lights. Mrs. Buckle walked onstage with her clipboard. There was a microphone set up in the middle with a spotlight shining on it.

"I'm so pleased that my class can share their talents with you today," said Mrs. Buckle. "Please welcome our first performer, Newton!"

"That's my brother!" cried a little voice.

Everyone laughed.

Grace watched her classmates take the stage, one by one.

Jack's act was the longest. He jumped around, punching and kicking, until he knocked over the microphone with a loud bang.

"Very energetic, Jack!" said Mrs. Buckle. "Trixie and Spork, you're next. We're ready for some magic!"

Trixie swept onstage in her purple cape. She didn't even look at Grace when she passed by. Spork ran up, too. He was wearing a silver hat and a bowtie.

"Ladies and gentlemen," began

Trixie. "Watch as I give this ordinary piece of chewing gum to my assistant."

Trixie passed Spork a piece of gum. He popped it into his mouth.

"Hocus pocus!" Trixie called. *"Bubble appear! Come out of my helper's EAR!"*

The audience gasped as a pink bubble swelled from Spork's left ear. Spork acted as surprised as everyone else.

"WHOA!" said a fourth grader. "How'd you guys do that?"

"Magic," Trixie said.

Spork looked out at Grace. He gave her a quick wink. Grace winked back.

"That's not all," declared Trixie. "My assistant looks dashing. But I wish we matched. *Hocus pocus! Orange to grape. Make my helper match my cape!"*

No one but Grace noticed Spork holding his breath. But EVERYONE noticed when he started changing color. Orange, blue, green . . . purple!

"Ooooooh!" said the kindergartners.

"Glarps!" Spork said, pretending to be alarmed.

"Come on, Trixie. What's the secret?" Jack demanded.

"I told you," said Trixie. "Magic!

Now, for the final trick, I will ask my assistant to lie down on the stage."

Spork looked confused. "Wait, what's this part?"

"You'll see," said Trixie. "Lie down!"

She said another spell. *"Hocus pocus, don't hesitate. Make my helper LEVITATE!"*

Spork's body lifted off the floor! He hovered in the air, as high as Trixie's knees!

"Spork, I didn't know you could float like that!" cried Grace, forgetting all about the act.

"*I CAN'T!*" squeaked Spork. "WHAT'S HAPPENING?"

Trixie smiled mysteriously. "Magic," she said again.

Then she dropped something from her fingers. *POOF!* A cloud of sparkly smoke filled the air. When it cleared, Spork was back on his feet. Trixie grabbed his hand, and they took a bow.

The audience went wild, whistling and cheering!

Then Grace heard another sound, even louder than the crowd.

WEEEET! WEEEET! WEEEET!

The fire alarm!

5

THE SHOW MUST GO ON

Grace made her way outside with her class. Soon the whole school was standing on the lawn. Mrs. Buckle went to talk to Principal Hale.

Trixie groaned. "What a mess. I didn't think that trick smoke would set off the alarm."

"It's my fault," Spork said miserably. "I'm bad luck! Every time I do an act, something goes wrong. I'll never be in a talent show again!"

WEE-OOO! WEE-OOO! A fire engine roared up.

Three firefighters ran into the school. A few minutes later, they trotted back out.

"Grilled cheese!" called the chief.

"Excuse me?" said Principal Hale.

Mrs. Reese gasped. "Oh, dear! The show was so good, I forgot all about the grilled cheese sandwiches I was making. I must have set off the alarm!"

"You mean, it wasn't my fault?" Spork said.

"Or mine? *Phew!*" said Trixie. She grinned at Grace for a second. Then she frowned.

"There's no damage. Except to the sandwiches!" said the chief. "You can go inside."

Grace hoped Principal Hale would send everyone straight to their classrooms. If the rest of the show was cancelled, she wouldn't have to sing!

But Principal Hale said, "Back to the cafeteria. The show must go on!"

Inside, kids were buzzing away about the magic tricks. And the sparkly smoke. And the fire truck! How could anyone follow all that excitement?

Grace saw Mrs. Buckle's clipboard on the table. She picked it up. There was only one act left in the show. Hers!

I can't do it! Grace thought. *I have to tell Mrs. Buckle.*

Then she heard her teacher's voice over the microphone. "Our final performer will sing a song. Please welcome . . . Grace!"

Oh, no.

Grace felt as if her feet belonged to someone else. Somehow, they began shuffling toward the stage.

She heard her classmates whisper as she went by.

"*Grace* is going to sing?" Jack said. "Seriously?"

"I didn't even know she liked to sing," said Newton.

"Me neither," said Trixie. "And I'm her best friend!"

Grace stood at the microphone. The spotlight felt hot and bright.

She looked out at the crowd, but she couldn't see their faces. Everything was swimming in front of her eyes. Her heart was banging hard.

It's okay to feel afraid, she told herself. *Be brave!*

She thought of Malavath, standing on top of the mountain.

She thought of herself singing in her room, feeling as if she could fly.

Grace took a shaky breath.

"O beautiful, for spacious skies." Her voice was soft and trembly. But she kept going. *"For amber waves of grain."*

Grace closed her eyes. She felt her fear start to melt away. *"For purple mountain majesties . . ."*

Before long, she wasn't scared at all.

She was flying. She was *soaring!*

Her voice rang out, strong and clear, all the way to the last line of the song. With her eyes still closed, Grace raised her arms to the sky.

"From sea to shining SEA!"

She did it. *She did it!*

Grace opened her eyes. She could see the audience just fine now.

They had funny looks on their faces. The room was silent.

I thought it was good. But maybe it wasn't, thought Grace. *Maybe it was awful!*

Then Trixie jumped up. "HOORAY!" she cried, clapping wildly.

Spork stood up, too. So did everyone else! Soon all the kids and teachers were applauding.

It was a standing ovation!

Grace couldn't believe it. She barely had time to take a bow before her class rushed onstage. Everyone wanted to hug her. Even Jack. And Trixie!

"Thank you for coming to our show!" Mrs. Buckle told the crowd. Then she ran over to hug Grace, too.

"Is that kind of singing ordinary on Earth?" asked Spork. "On my planet, it would be *extraordinary*!"

"It's extraordinary here, too," said Mrs. Buckle. She brushed a tear from her cheek. "Grace, that was *lovely*. I had no idea you took voice lessons."

"I don't," said Grace. She felt shy again. "That's the first time I ever sang in front of anyone."

"Wow!" said Newton. "That was brave!"

"Especially when your best friend wasn't on your side," said Trixie. "I'm sorry, Grace. I should have listened to what you wanted. Can you forgive me?"

"YES!" said Grace. It felt great to have Trixie back—as great as all the applause in the world.

"Hey, next year we can sing *together* in the talent show!" Trixie said. "I'll be the lead singer, and—" Trixie stopped. "No, *you* be the lead singer, Grace. I'll sing back-up."

"I like that plan," said Grace.

"Awesome!" said Trixie. "Now, here's what we'll wear. . . ."

Over Trixie's shoulder, Grace saw Spork wink.

Grace winked back.

REPORT TO TROOP

BEEP. BEEP. BEEP.
Guys, I was in the talent show—and nothing went wrong! Well, the fire department came. But that wasn't my fault. Really!
And my act was a HIT!
I can't wait for the next Galaxy Scouts show. I'm thinking archery. Who wants me to shoot a zapple off their head? Come on, guys, be brave! How about you, Nerp? Or you, Dwyz?
Guys? GUYS?

ACTIVITIES

Greetings!
Are you brave? I used to think I wasn't, because whenever I had to do something scary, my antennae twitched like crazy! But guess what? I found out being brave doesn't mean you're not afraid. It means you do stuff even though you ARE afraid! Take this quick quiz and test your Courage I.Q.
—Spork

(There can be more than one right answer.)

1. You *love* playing yubble, and you really want to try out for the team. But you're nervous. So you:
   a. Run straight home and hide under your bed.
   b. Ask a friend to go to the tryouts with you.
   c. Let yourself be nervous . . . and try out anyway.
   d. Tell the coach you shouldn't have to try out since you already won a gold medal at the Interplanetary Olympics. Hope he doesn't check.

2. You *hate* the Tummy Twister at the Galaxy Fair, and you *don't* want to ride it. But your friends might think you're a scaredy-flarg. So you:
   a. Get on the ride and prepare to lose your lunch.
   b. Distract your friends. ("Hey, look—free candy!")
   c. Say, "I don't like this ride, but I'll wait while you guys go."
   d. Skip the whole fair.

3. You walk around at school one day with toilet paper stuck to your shoe. Everyone sees it and laughs! What should you do?

   a. Never go back to school. *Ever.*

   b. Go to school the next day disguised as a new student from the planet Megbar.

   c. Go to school and stick toilet paper to someone else's shoe—that way *they'll* get laughed at.

   d. Go to school and act normal.

4. Your friend's mom offers you a food you've never tried—boiled Yorgnak. What should you do?

   a. Take a tiny taste. Hey, you might even like it.

   b. Scrape it onto your friend's plate when no one's looking.

   c. Say, "No, thank you."

   d. Say, "Ew! That looks GROSS!"

Answers:

1. *B* and *c* are both great answers. It always helps to have backup, so bringing a buddy along is smart. And it's okay to get the jitters. Take a deep breath of fresh Earth air and give it your best shot!

2. Just thinking about answer *a* makes my stomach hurt! Don't do something you don't want to do just to look brave. It's actually braver to be honest, like in answer *c*. You could pick *d*, but then you'd miss all the fun . . . and the Fried Flickles on a Stick!

3. Oh, boy—it takes *a lot* of courage to bounce back from something embarrassing. It's tempting to pick *a*, *b*, or *c*, isn't it? But *d* is the best answer. Sure, people might tease you when you get back to school. But if you smile and shrug it off, they'll forget about your toilet paper troubles.

4. If you pick *d*, you won't get invited back any time soon. And *b* could backfire if you get busted! *C* is a fine option. But why not go for *a?* If you take a bite and you don't like it, you can spit it out in your napkin. As long as you do it quietly, it's not considered rude (except on the planet Megbar—and that's just because they don't have napkins).

Space Facts: True or False

This little test has helped me on my Galaxy Scout mission to Earth. And believe me, in this neighborhood you have to be as sharp as a vorfy blade! See how you do.

1. Mars has the highest mountain of any planet in Earth's solar system.
2. A chicken was the first Earth creature to travel in space.
3. There's lots of junk orbiting Earth. Don't get hit!
4. Venus is a nice place to visit.
5. From space, the brightest city on Earth is Las Vegas.
6. Uda is the only square planet.
7. There are moons called Io, Ariel, and Frank.
8. Scientists have heard strange music coming from Neptune.

Answers:

1. True. It's three times taller than Mount Everest!

2. False. But lots of other Earth creatures have visited space—like fish, frogs, snails, dogs, cats, and monkeys! So what did go to space first? Fruit flies!

3. True. There are more than 500,000 pieces of junk in space, some smaller than a bug and some bigger than a bus! It's mostly parts of spaceships or satellites, but there's also a glove and a camera dropped by astronauts.

4. False. Venus is a rotten place to visit! It's sizzling hot (900 degrees!), plus the air is thick and full of poison. It's also got acid clouds and crazy winds like in Earth hurricanes. I didn't have a very good vacation there.

5. True. It looks very pretty!

6. False. There are no square planets—and no planet Uda either.

7. False. No moons are named Frank. But there *are* moons called Io and Ariel, plus moons named Kale, Cupid, Titan, Albiorix—and Margaret.

8. False. It's a joke! NepTUNES—get it?

MEET THE AUTHOR AND ILLUSTRATOR

LORI HASKINS HOURAN
has written more than twenty
books for kids (not counting
the ones her flarg ate). She
lives in Florida with two silly
aliens who claim to be her
sons.

JESSICA WARRICK has
illustrated lots of picture
books about dogs, cats,
and kids, but she is mostly
interested in drawing aliens,
for some strange reason. She
does a pretty good job acting
like an Earthling . . . most of
the time.

Spork just landed on Earth, and look, he already has lots of fans!

★ **Moonbeam Children's Book Awards Gold Medal**
Best Book Series—Chapter Books

★ **Moonbeam Children's Book Awards Silver Medal**
Juvenile Fiction—Early Reader/Chapter Books
for book #1 *Spork Out of Orbit*

"Young readers are going to love this series! Spork is a funny and unexpected main character. Kids will love his antics and sweet disposition. Teachers and parents will appreciate the subtle messages embedded in the stories. The kids in the stories genuinely like each other, which I found refreshing. I will be giving these books to my young friends."—**Ron Roy**, author of A to Z Mysteries, Calendar Mysteries, and Capital Mysteries

"A breezy, humorous lesson in honesty that never stoops to didacticism. The other three volumes publishing simultaneously address similarly weighty lessons—lying, shyness, bullying, and responsibility—all with a multicultural cast of Everykids. . . . A good choice for those new to chapters."
—**Kirkus** for book #1 *Spork Out of Orbit*

"This is a book where readers, kids, and aliens learn together, experiencing how words and choices affect all of us. It's simple, elegant, and very insightful storytelling. *Greetings, Sharkling!* doesn't waste a single page of opportunity."
—**The San Francisco Book Review**

"I'm so glad Spork landed on Earth! His misadventures are playful and sweet, and I love the clever wordplay!"
—**Becca Zerkin**, former children's book reviewer for the *New York Times Book Review* and *School Library Journal*

"Kids will love reading about Spork. Parents, teachers, and librarians will love reading aloud this series to those same kids."—**Rob Reid**, author of *Silly Books to Read Aloud*

How to Be an Earthling
Winner of the Moonbeam Gold Medal
for Best Chapter Book Series!

Respect

Honesty

Responsibility

Courage

Kindness

Perseverance

Citizenship

Self-Control

Check out these other series from Kane Press